BEN 10 ALIEN FORCE™

TRIPLE THREAT

By Tracey West

SCHOLASTIC INC.

New York   Toronto   London   Auckland
Sydney   Mexico City   New Delhi   Hong Kong

ISBN: 978-0-545-17717-7

CARTOON NETWORK, the logo, BEN 10 ALIEN FORCE,
and all related characters and elements are trademarks of and
© 2010 Cartoon Network.
Published by Scholastic Inc.
SCHOLASTIC and associated logos are trademarks and/or
registered trademarks of Scholastic Inc.

12 11 10 9 8 7 6 5 4 3 2   40   10 11 12 13 14/0

Illustrations by Min Sung Ku and Hi-Fi Design
Printed in the U.S.A.
First printing, January 2010

"You missed a spot, Ben," Kevin said.

Ben was polishing the hood of Kevin's car. "Come on, Kevin. I only spilled, like, a drop of smoothy on it. It's clean!"

"Keep going," Kevin told him. "This is the most beautiful car in the world, and I want it to stay that way."

Gwen clicked her cell phone shut.
"Sorry, Kev, but we've got to go," she said.
"That was Grandpa Max. He's got an emergency
assignment for us."

Ben, Gwen, and Kevin climbed into the car and headed for Plumbers HQ. The Plumbers protected the galaxy from intergalactic criminals. Grandpa Max was in charge of Earth's quadrant. "What's going on, Gramps?" Ben asked.

"We've detected an alien spy transmitter somewhere in the Blackrock Mountains," Max said. "I need you to locate and deactivate it. It's protected by a cloaking device."

"The Blackrock Mountains?" Gwen asked. "I've heard stories about people vanishing there. They're never heard from again."

Max nodded. "That's why I'm sending you three out there. You're my best team."

Suddenly, a voice came from the doorway. "If you guys don't want the assignment, we'll take it," said Pierce.

Pierce, Helen, and Manny were a team of Plumbers-in-training.

"We never said we didn't want it," Kevin said.

"Yeah, it's no problem," added Ben. "We've dealt with a lot worse than some mysterious mountains."

"Can we look for the transmitter, too?" Pierce asked Max.

Grandpa Max shrugged. "Sure. I don't care who takes down that transmitter. I just want it done. You'll probably want to grab that anti-cloaking device from the—"

Before he could finish, Manny and Kevin were racing down the hall to the equipment room.

"You guys should give up now," Kevin said. "There's no way you can win this."

"Oh yeah?" Manny replied. He skidded to a stop and grinned.

Helen zipped past them both. She darted into the equipment room and grabbed the anti-cloaking device.

Manny, Helen, and Pierce jumped into their truck and drove off.

Kevin raced for his car. "Move it, guys!" he called to Ben and Gwen.

Ben shook his head. "Kevin, this doesn't have to be a race!"

"Yes it does," said Kevin. "No way am I going to lose to those rookies."

"Kevin, this isn't just about speed," Gwen told him. "We need a strategy." She showed Ben her laptop screen. "People get lost in the Blackrocks all the time. I located a map of the mountain trails and calculated the most likely spot for a transmitter."

"But what about the anti-cloaking device?" Ben asked.

"It only works within a twenty-foot distance," Gwen explained. "Trust me. Manny, Helen, and Pierce will be wandering around lost while we deactivate the transmitter."

Suddenly . . . *POP!* The car spun off the road.

"Oh, that's just great," Kevin moaned. "We blew a tire!"

"Tell you what," Ben said. "You fix this. I'll keep an eye on them."

He dialed up his Omnitrix. "Jet Ray!" he cried, transforming into a red alien with long arms and yellow wings.

Jet Ray flew after the truck. He found Manny, Helen, and Pierce setting up camp at the base of the mountains.

Kevin and Gwen met Ben at a nearby diner.

"I think they're going to head out in the morning," Ben told them. He looked at the map Gwen had printed out. "That's what we should do, too. We can head up this trail and—"

Whoosh! Helen raced past him, grabbing the map out of his hands!

"Now they've gone too far!" Kevin said angrily. He ran out of the diner, touching a car as he passed. His whole body turned to steel.

Slam! He tackled Manny before Manny could get back in the truck.

Manny pushed him back.

Gwen aimed a blast of pink energy at each of them. The energy bubbles carried them up in the air, away from each other.

"We're on the same side, remember?" she said.

"You're right, Gwen," said Helen. "I shouldn't have taken the map. Here, it's yours."

"Keep it," Ben said. "I'm calling a truce.
Let's meet at the trail head at seven. Deal?"

Pierce nodded and shook Ben's hand.
"Deal," he said.

Gwen set down Manny and Kevin. They
eyed each other and grunted.

"I hope you know what you're doing, Ben,"
Kevin muttered.

Ben, Gwen, and Kevin camped out that night. They
got to the meeting place at seven. But Manny's truck
wasn't there.

"Check out those tire tracks," Gwen said, pointing
up the trail. "Guess they started without us."

"I knew it!" Kevin cried.

Kevin sped up the twisting mountain road. Suddenly, Gwen put her hand on the steering wheel.

"Slow down!" she said. "I'm sensing some energy up ahead. Really, really big energy."

They turned a bend and drove right into a giant alien!

The huge creature towered over Manny, Helen, and Pierce.

Pierce shot sharp quills at it. Manny blasted it with all four of his laser guns. Helen raced around and around it, trying to knock it down. But the creature brushed them off like they were harmless flies.

Ben slammed his palm down on the Omnitrix.
His body glowed as it transformed into a huge,
dinosaurlike alien. "Humungousaur!" he bellowed.
Humungousaur picked up the giant slug.
Manny, Helen, and Pierce ran to safety.

"Aaaaiiiiiiiieeeeeee!" The slug twisted in Humungousaur's arms, then shot a wave of sticky green slime out of its mouth.

"Toxic!" Humungousaur yelled. He dropped the slug.

The slug aimed a blast of the toxic slime at Gwen and Kevin. Gwen quickly created a pink energy shield. The slime hit it and slid harmlessly to the ground.

The slug reared up for another attack, then stopped. It started to slither toward Kevin's car.

"What's it doing?" Kevin asked.

"They're the same color," Gwen pointed out. "Maybe it thinks your car is a friend."

Kevin looked at Manny. "Give me some cover?"

Manny nodded. "You got it!"

Kevin raced toward his car. Manny shot laser blasts at the slug as Kevin jumped into the driver's seat.

"Hey, Slimy! Follow me!" Kevin called.

"He's buying us time to find the transmitter,"
Gwen said.

"I'm on it," said Helen. She held up the anti-
cloaking device.

Helen zoomed around the area. Soon there
was a bright light, and the transmitter appeared.

"My turn," said Humungousaur. He stomped
on the transmitter, breaking it.

Meanwhile, the alien slug was giving Kevin's car a big, slimy hug. Humungousaur pulled the car out of the slug's grasp. Then Manny aimed his lasers at a cliff above the slug.

The rocks came crashing down, trapping the slug.
Ben transformed back into his human form. "Let's get out of here!"

Back at Plumbers HQ, Grandpa Max was happy to hear that the transmitter had been destroyed.

"Everyone learned to work together," Ben said.

Pierce nodded. "Yeah, it was a good team effort."

"Actually, *we* did most of the work," said Manny.

Kevin clenched his fists. "Are you kidding me? We saved you from that giant slime ball, remember?"

"Hey, guys. How about we grab a pizza to celebrate?" Helen suggested.

Kevin frowned. "Maybe some other time. I've got something I need to do."

It took hours for Kevin to scrub the alien slime off of his car.

"You know, you're right, Kevin," Ben joked. "This really is the most beautiful car in the world—if you're an alien slug!"